A Collecti

Bedtime Stories

for Kids

Relaxing Reading for Little Ones, Fantasy
Fables for Children for Promote a Healthy
Sleep

Clara Farrell

Table of Contents

solely under their purview. There are no scenarios in which the publisher or the original author of this work can be in any fashion deemed liable for any hardship or damages that may befall them after undertaking information described herein.

Additionally, the information in the following pages is intended only for informational purposes and should thus be thought of as universal. As befitting its nature, it is presented without assurance regarding its prolonged validity or interim quality. Trademarks that are mentioned are done without written consent and can in no way be considered an endorsement from the trademark holder.

Introduction

Reading is the most important thing we can teach our children, reading is as essential today as breathing. Children will not be able to survive nowadays if they don't know how to read. We all know that learning and education begins at home. Parents should try to teach their kids how to read as soon as possible to provide them an edge when its time for them to go to school.

One way of encouraging kids to read is to read to them, the bedtime stories our parents use to read to us are not only to entertain us before we go to sleep but to also encourage us to learn how to read. Research shows that kids who read to by their parents when they were young are better at reading and studying.

Now as parents are duty is to provide reading materials to our kids that are tailored made for them. Reading materials that will encourage our kids not just to read, but learn about new things and acquire extra knowledge like about animals and their natural habitats. There are a lot of materials out there we can give our kids to encourage them to read. There are books, games, toys and many more that we can give them. But as we know, kids today have a very short attention span, if the thing we provide them does not interest them or intimidate them they will not even spend five minutes with it. Books are a good source of material that we can give to our kids, but most of the time kids find books intimidating and really boring because of the lack of visual materials. Kids learn better and faster if they have visual stimulation.

The art of telling a good bedtime story dates back quite far. This remarkable discovery speaks volumes as to the importance of telling bedtime stories to your child. Parents for literally thousands of years have told variations of the stories told today. It is an oral tradition of great importance and one that all parents should be doing. Not only is a bedtime story fun and relaxing, it is also an effective and important way to become closer with your child.

What Is a Bedtime Story?

Bedtime stories are stories that are told after your child has gotten into bed for the evening. Many times they will ask for you to sit with them. This is an easy opportunity to offer to tell them a story. Young children especially love this because it is a treat for them and makes them feel truly important at that moment.

You can either read a classic story from a book, find a quick one online, or tell one from memory. Oftentimes a great bedtime story is improvised to suit the mood of your child in that particular moment. These stories are typically ones that have been told for many years in many different ways. Popular stories include ones about princesses and princes, great monsters and knights, children on adventures, and exciting tales with no particular ending to them. This latter type of story is interesting because it allows you to draw the same story out over many nights to keep your child interested and always wanting more.

Develop Memories Together

Reading a bedtime story to your children is a great way to connect with them. It brings the family closer in an intimate setting that also makes the child feel special. Memories are made as stories are told. Your child will look forward to you sitting with them before they drift off to sleep. This time together is something that they will always cherish. These precious moments benefit everyone involved, and you will find that you look forward to the bedtime stories almost as much, or more than your little one.

Benefits Of Bedtime Stories

Telling bedtime stories is beneficial. Your child will find sleep coming in a peaceful way with a great story in their ears. It engages their imagination while giving them good dream material, and has been shown to calm down a busy child. Children do tend to be worked up at times, especially at night, and a nice story will put their fears to rest and allow them much-needed relaxation. You can make a story that shows them that the monster under their bed is not so bad, or that the shadows on their wall are their friends. The possibilities are endless with creative solutions to any nighttime issue.

Bedtime stories also teach your child in ways that are similar to fables, myths, and fairy tales. Reading bedtime stories is a compelling way of helping your child grow into a well-shaped individual. The fun part about bedtime stories is that you can make one up yourself and craft it into something unique and special. A special story goes a long way for a child with open ears, and you will become a source of great interest to your children.

Christmas Stories

There is no time of the year quite like Christmas. This holiday is a great time to read classic stories to your child. The amount of Christmas stories out there is immense. No matter your background, tradition, or culture you will find stories that can find an important home in your children's mind during the holiday season.

Well-known Christmas stories include:

- A Christmas Carol
- The Snowman
- Rudolf the Red-Nosed Reindeer
- 'Twas the Night Before Christmas

In different cultures, there are Christmas stories with different flavors, but similar messages of charity, family, love, and tradition. Some examples include:

- The Story of Babushka (Russia)
- Santa Kullosu (South Korea)
- Bom Velhinho (Brazil)

Why Tell Christmas Stories

The importance of Christmas stories lies in the messages that they share.

Regardless of creed, culture, or country, there are universal messages to be taken from Christmas. This special holiday celebrates life, family, tradition, and community. Each of these elements wraps into a nice package that a child will enjoy.

Christmas stories teach children about the importance of giving to others. This shapes them for future interactions with other children, and as they grow, with other adults. They will also learn about why being close to family is something to cherish. This holiday period brings the family together, and children can benefit greatly from these stories.

Benefits of Christmas Stories

Benefits of reading or telling Christmas stories are many.

You will connect with your child with genuine quality time. Having a tight family unit has been shown to increase a child's self-esteem, self-value, and empathy for others. Research also says that bonding as a family helps a child's emotional and academic development.

Your child will associate this time of year with giving, love, sharing, and closeness. Having a strong tradition such as a Christmas storytime will teach your child to associate the holidays with positive behavior rather than asking for more toys and such. Reading classic stories is a great way to shift the focus to more important values.

Your child will have his or her imagination excited in the best way possible. It almost goes without saying that stimulating a child's creativity, imagination, and mental faculties are of the utmost importance. Telling stories of magical reindeer, a jolly old man delivering gifts to all the children of the world, and of talking snowmen will bring joy to your young one.

Bringing The Family Together

When the Christmas holidays do roll around, be sure to engage in activities that bring your family together. Out of the many things you can do as a family, such as baking, watching old films, wrapping gifts, and cooking, you can sit down and read stories to your child.

This creates a tradition of family time that you can do each year. Your child will come to look forward to this, perhaps even more than the idea of gifts. Be sure to supplement the storytelling and book reading with the watching of classic movies such as:

- A Christmas Story
- White Christmas
- A Christmas Carol
- 'Twas the Night Before Christmas
- 'Twas the night before Christmas, when all through the house

Santa and the Poor Daughters

Baron Derbyshire was a kindly nobleman whose life was extremely hard. His beloved wife had died of an illness leaving him and his three daughters in utter despair.

After losing all his money in useless and bad inventions the family had to move from their castle in Yorkshire, England, into a peasant's cottage, where the daughters did their own cooking, sewing, and cleaning. When it came time for the daughters to marry, Baron Derbyshire became even more depressed as his daughters could not marry without dowries, money, and property given to the new husband's family.

One night after the daughters had washed their clothing they hung their stockings over the fireplace to dry. That night Saint Nicholas, knowing the despair of the father, stopped by the nobleman's hovel. Looking in at the window Saint Nicholas saw that the family had already gone to bed. He also noticed the daughters stockings. Saint Nicholas was profoundly moved and he took three small bags of gold from his pouch and threw them one by one down the chimney whereupon they landed in the stockings.

The next morning when the daughters awoke they found their stockings contained enough gold for them to get married. Baron Derbyshire was able to see his three daughters marry, and he lived a long and happy life.

A Letter from Santa Claus

Palace of Saint Nicholas in the Moon Christmas Morning

My Dear Susy Clemens,

I have received and read all the letters which you and your little sister have written me . . . . I can read your and your baby sister's jagged and fantastic marks without any trouble at all. But I had trouble with those letters which you dictated through your mother and the nurses, for I am a foreigner and cannot read English writing well. You will find that I made no mistakes about the things which you and the baby ordered in your own letters--I went down your chimney at midnight when you were asleep and delivered them all myself--and kissed both of you, too. But there were one or two small orders which I could not fill because we ran out of stock .

There was a word or two in your mama's letter which I took to be "a trunk full of doll's clothes." Is that it? I will call at your kitchen door about nine o'clock this morning to inquire. But I must not see anybody and I must not speak to anybody but you. When the kitchen doorbell rings, George must be blindfolded and sent to the door. You must tell George he must walk on tiptoe and not speak-- otherwise, he will die someday. Then you must go up to the nursery and stand on a chair or the nurse's bed and put your ear to the speaking tube that leads down to the kitchen and when I whistle through it you must speak in the tube and say, "Welcome, Santa Claus!" Then I will ask whether it was a trunk you ordered or not. If you say it was, I shall ask you what color you want the trunk to be and then you must tell me every single thing in detail which you want the trunk to contain. Then when I say "Good-by and a merry Christmas to my little Susy Clemens," you must say "Good-by, good old Santa Claus, I thank you very much." Then you must go down into the library and make George close all the doors that open into the main hall, and everybody must keep still for a little while. I will go to the moon and get those things and in a few minutes I will come down the chimney that belongs to the fireplace that is in the hall--if it is a trunk you want--because I couldn't get such a thing as a trunk down the nursery chimney, you know. If I should leave any snow in the hall, you must tell George to sweep it into the fireplace, for I haven't time to do such things. George must not use a broom, but a rag--else he will die someday. If my boot should leave a stain on the marble, George must not holystone it away. Leave it there always in memory of my visit, and whenever you look at it or show it to anybody you must let it remind you to be a good little girl. Whenever you are naughty and someone points to that mark which your good old Santa Claus's boot made on the marble, what will you say, little sweetheart?

The Night After Christmas

'TWAS the night after Christmas, and all through the house

Not a creature was stirring—excepting a mouse.

The stockings were flung in haste over the chair,

For hopes of St. Nicholas were no longer there.

The children were restlessly tossing in bed,

For the pie and the candy were heavy as lead;

While mamma in her kerchief, and I in my gown,

Had just made up our minds that we would not lie down,

When out on the lawn there arose such a clatter,

I sprang from my chair to see what was the matter.

Away to the window, I went with a dash,

Flung open the shutter and threw up the sash.

The moon on the breast of the new-fallen snow,

Gave the luster of noon-day to objects below,

When what to my long anxious eyes should appear

But a horse and a sleigh, both old-fashioned and queer;

With a little old driver, so solemn and slow,

I knew at a glance it must be Dr. Brough.

—

I drew in my head, and was turning around,

When upstairs came the Doctor, with scarcely a sound.

He wore a thick overcoat, made long ago,

And the beard on his chin was white with the snow. I drew

in my head, and was turning around,

When upstairs came the Doctor, with scarcely a sound.

He wore a thick overcoat, made long ago,

And the beard on his chin was white with the snow.

He spoke a few words, and went straight to his work;

He felt all the pulses,—then turned with a jerk,

And laying his finger aside of his nose,

With a nod of his head to the chimney he goes:—

"A spoonful of oil, ma'am, if you have it handy;

No nuts and no raisins, no pies and no candy.

These tender young stomachs cannot well digest

All the sweets that they get; toys and books are the best.

But I know my advice will not find many friends,

For the custom of Christmas, the other way tends.

The fathers and mothers, and Santa Claus, too,

Are exceedingly blind. Well, a good-night to you!"

And I heard him exclaim, as he drove out of sight:

"These feastings and candies make Doctors' bills right!"

The Fir Tree

FAR down in the forest, where the warm sun and the fresh air made a sweet resting-place, grew a pretty little fir-tree; and yet it was not happy, it wished so much to be tall like its companions the pines and firs which grew around it.

The sun shone, and the soft air fluttered its leaves, and the little peasant children passed by, prattling merrily, but the fir-tree heeded them not. Sometimes the children would bring a large basket of raspberries or strawberries, wreathed on a straw, and seat themselves near the fir-tree, and say, "Is it not a pretty little tree?" which made it feel more unhappy than before. And yet all this while the tree grew a notch or joint taller every year; for by the number of joints in the stem of a fir-tree we can discover its age.

Still, as it grew, it complained, "Oh! how I wish I were as tall as the other trees, then I would spread out my branches on every side, and my top would over-look the wide world. I should have the birds building their nests on my boughs, and when the wind blew, I should bow with stately dignity like my tall companions."

The tree was so discontented, that it took no pleasure in the warm sunshine, the birds, or the rosy clouds that floated over it morning and evening. Sometimes, in winter, when the snow lay white and glittering on the ground, a hare would come springing along, and jump right over the little tree; and then how mortified it would feel! Two winters passed, and when the third arrived, the tree had grown so tall that the hare was obliged to run around it.

Yet it remained unsatisfied, and would exclaim, "Oh if I could but keep on growing tall and old! There is nothing else worth caring for in the world!"

In the autumn, as usual, the wood-cutters came and cut down several of the tallest trees, and the young fir-tree, which was now grown to its full height, shuddered as the noble trees fell to the earth with a crash. After the branches were lopped off, the trunks looked so slender and bare, that they could scarcely be recognized. Then they were placed upon wagons and drawn by horses out of the forest.

"Where were they going? What would become of them?" The young fir-tree wished very much to know; so in the spring, when the swallows and the storks came, it asked, "Do you know where those trees were taken? Did you meet them?"

The swallows knew nothing, but the stork, after a little reflection, nodded his head, and said, "Yes, I think I do. I met several new ships when I flew from Egypt, and they had fine masts that smelt like fir. I think these must have been the trees; I assure you they were stately, very stately."

"Oh, how I wish I were tall enough to go on the sea," said the fir-tree. "What is the sea, and what does it look like?"

"It would take too much time to explain," said the stork, flying quickly away.

"Rejoice in thy youth," said the sunbeam; "rejoice in thy fresh growth, and the young life that is in thee." And the wind kissed the tree, and the dew watered it with tears, but the fir-tree regarded them not.

Christmas-time drew near, and many young trees were cut down, some even smaller and younger than the fir-tree who enjoyed neither rest nor peace with longing to leave its forest home. These young trees, which were chosen for their beauty, kept their branches and were also laid on wagons and drawn by horses out of the forest.

"Where are they going?" asked the fir-tree. "They are not taller than I am: indeed, one is much less; and why are the branches not cut off? Where are they going?"

"We know, we know," sang the sparrows; "we have looked in at the windows of the houses in the town, and we know what is done with them. They are dressed up in the most splendid manner. We have seen them standing in the middle of a warm room, and adorned with all sorts of beautiful things,- honey cakes, gilded apples, playthings, and many hundreds of wax tapers."

"And then," asked the fir-tree, trembling through all its branches, "and then what happens?"

"We did not see anymore," said the sparrows; "but this was enough for us."

"I wonder whether anything so brilliant will ever happen to me," thought the fir-tree. "It would be much better than crossing the sea. I long for it almost with pain. Oh! when will Christmas be here? I am now as tall and well grown as those which were taken away last year. Oh! that I were now laid on the wagon, or standing in the warm room, with all that brightness and splendor around me! Something better and more beautiful is to come after, or the trees would not be so decked out. Yes, what follows will be grander and more splendid. What can it be? I am weary with longing. I scarcely know how I feel."

"Rejoice with us," said the air and the sunlight. "Enjoy thine own bright life in the fresh air."

But the tree would not rejoice, though it grew taller every day; and, winter and summer, its dark-green foliage might be seen in the forest, while passers-by would say, "What a beautiful tree!" A short time before Christmas, the discontented fir-tree was the first to fall.

As the axe cut through the stem and divided the pith, the tree fell with a groan to the earth, conscious of pain and faintness, and forgetting all its anticipations of happiness, in sorrow at leaving its home in the forest. It knew that it should never again see its dear old companions, the trees, nor the little bushes and many-colored flowers that had grown by its side; perhaps not even the birds. Neither was the journey at all pleasant. The tree first recovered itself while being unpacked in the courtyard of a house, with several other trees; and it heard a man say, "We only want one, and this is the prettiest." Then came two servants in grand livery, and carried the fir-tree into a large and beautiful apartment. On the walls hung pictures, and near the great stove stood great china vases, with lions on the lids. There were rocking chairs, silken sofas, large tables, covered with pictures, books, and playthings, worth a great deal of money,- at least, the children said so. Then the fir-tree was placed in a large tub, full of sand; but green baize hung all around it so that no one could see it was a tub, and it stood on a very handsome carpet. How the fir-tree trembled!

"What was going to happen to him now?"

Some young ladies came, and the servants helped them to adorn the tree. On one branch they hung little bags cut out of colored paper, and each bag was filled with sweetmeats; from other branches hung gilded apples and walnuts, as if they had grown there; and above, and all-round, were hundreds of red, blue, and white tapers, which were fastened on the branches. Dolls, exactly like real babies, were placed under the green leaves,- the tree had never seen such things before,- and at the very top was fastened a glittering star, made of tinsel. Oh, it was very beautiful!

"This evening," they all exclaimed, "how bright it will be!"

"Oh, that the evening came," thought the tree, "and the tapers lighted! then I shall know what else is going to happen. Will the trees of the forest come to see me? I wonder if the sparrows will peep in at the windows as they fly? Shall I grow faster here, and keep on all these ornaments summer and winter?"

But guessing was of very little use; it made his bark ache, and this pain is as bad for a slender fir-tree, as headache is for us. At last, the tapers were lighted, and then what a glistening blaze of light the tree presented! It trembled so with joy in all its branches, that one of the candles fell among the green leaves and burnt some of them.

"Help! help!" exclaimed the young ladies, but there was no danger, for they quickly extinguished the fire. After this, the tree tried not to tremble at all, though the fire frightened him; he was so anxious not to hurt any of the beautiful ornaments, even while their brilliancy dazzled him. And now the folding doors were thrown open, and a troop of children rushed in as if they intended to upset the tree; they were followed more silently by their elders. For a moment the little ones stood silent with astonishment, and then they shouted for joy, till the room rang, and they danced merrily round the tree, while one present after another was taken from it.

"What are they doing? What will happen next?" thought the fir.

At last, the candles burnt down to the branches and were put out. Then the children received permission to plunder the tree. Oh, how they rushed upon it, till the branches cracked, and had it not been fastened with the glistening star to the ceiling, it must have been thrown down. The children then danced about with their pretty toys, and no one noticed the tree, except the children's maid who came and peeped among the branches to see if an apple or a fig had been forgotten.

"A story, a story," cried the children, pulling a little fat man towards the tree.

"Now we shall be in the green shade," said the man, as he seated himself under it, "and the tree will have the pleasure of hearing also, but I shall only relate one story; what shall it be? IvedeAvede, or Humpty Dumpty, who fell downstairs, but soon got up again, and at last married a princess."

"Ivede-Avede," cried some.

"Humpty Dumpty," cried others, and there was a fine shouting and crying out.

But the fir-tree remained quite still, and thought to himself, "Shall I have anything to do with all this?" but he had already amused them as much as they wished. Then the old man told them the story of Humpty Dumpty, how he fell downstairs, and was raised up again, and married a princess. And the children clapped their hands and cried, "Tell another, tell another," for they wanted to hear the story of "Ivede-Avede;" but they only had

"Humpty Dumpty."

After this, the fir-tree became quite silent and thoughtful; never had the birds in the forest told such tales as "Humpty Dumpty," who fell downstairs and yet married a princess. "Ah! yes, so it happens in the world," thought the fir-tree; he believed it all because it was related by such a nice man. "Ah! well," he thought, "who knows? perhaps I may fall down too, and marry a princess;" and he looked forward joyfully to the next evening, expecting to be again decked out with lights and playthings, gold and fruit. "To-morrow I will not tremble," thought he; "I will enjoy all my splendor, and I shall hear the story of Humpty Dumpty again, and perhaps Ivede-Avede." And the tree remained quiet and thoughtful all night. In the morning the servants and the housemaid came in. "Now," thought the fir, "all my splendor is going to begin again." But they dragged him out of the room and upstairs to the garret, and threw him on the floor, in a dark corner, where no daylight shone, and there they left him.

"What does this mean?" thought the tree, "what am I to do here? I can hear nothing in a place like this," and he had time enough to think, for days and nights passed and no one came near him, and when at last somebody did come, it was only to put away large boxes in a corner. So the tree was completely hidden from sight as if it had never existed. "It is winter now," thought the tree, "the ground is hard and covered with snow so that people cannot plant me. I shall be sheltered here, I dare say until spring comes. How thoughtful and kind everybody is to me! Still, I wish this place were not so dark, as well as lonely, with not even a little hare to look at. How pleasant it was out in the forest while the snow lay on the ground when the hare would run by, yes, and jump over me too, although I did not like it then. Oh! it is terrible lonely here."

"Squeak, squeak," said a little mouse, creeping cautiously towards the tree; then came another; and they both sniffed at the fir-tree and crept between the branches.

"Oh, it is very cold," said the little mouse, "or else we should be so comfortable here, shouldn't we, you old fir-tree?"

"I am not old," said the fir-tree, "there are many who are older than I am."

"Where do you come from? and what do you know?" asked the mice, who were full of curiosity. "Have you seen the most beautiful places in the world, and can you tell us all about them? And have you been in the storeroom, where cheeses lie on the shelf, and hams hang from the ceiling? One can run about on tallow candles there, and go in thin and come out fat."

"I know nothing of that place," said the fir-tree, "but I know the wood where the sun shines and the birds sing." And then the tree told the little mice all about its youth. They had never heard such an account in their lives; and after they had listened to it attentively, they said, "What a number of things you have seen? You must have been very happy."

"Happy!" exclaimed the fir-tree, and then as he reflected upon what he had been telling them, he said, "Ah, yes! after all those were happy days." But when he went on and related all about Christmas-eve, and how he had been dressed up with cakes and lights, the mice said, "How happy you must have been, you old fir-tree."

"I am not old at all," replied the tree, "I only came from the forest this winter, I am now checked in my growth."

"What splendid stories you can relate," said the little mice. And the next night four other mice came with them to hear what the tree had to tell.

The more he talked the more he remembered, and then he thought to himself, "Those were happy days, but they may come again. Humpty Dumpty fell downstairs, and yet he married the princess; perhaps I may marry a princess too." And the fir-tree thought of the pretty little birch-tree that grew in the forest, which was to him a real beautiful princess.

"Who is Humpty Dumpty?" asked the little mice. And then the tree related the whole story; he could remember every single word, and the little mice were so delighted with it, that they were ready to jump to the top of the tree. The next night a great many more mice made their appearance, and on Sunday two rats came with them; but they said, it was not a pretty story at all, and the little mice were very sorry, for it made them also think less of it.

"Do you know only one story?" asked the rats. "Only one," replied the fir-tree; "I heard it on the happiest evening of my life, but I did not know I was so happy at the time."

"We think it is a very miserable story," said the rats. "Don't you know any story about bacon or tallow in the storeroom."

"No," replied the tree.

"Many thanks to you then," replied the rats, and they marched off.

The little mice also kept away after this, and the tree sighed, and said, "It was very pleasant when the merry little mice sat round me and listened while I talked. Now that is all passed too. However, I shall consider myself happy when someone comes to take me out of this place. But would this ever happen?"

Yes; one morning people came to clear out the garret, the boxes were packed away, and the tree was pulled out of the corner, and thrown roughly on the garret floor; then the servant dragged it out upon the staircase where the daylight shone.

"Now life is beginning again," said the tree, rejoicing in the sunshine and fresh air. Then it was carried downstairs and taken into the courtyard so quickly, that it forgot to think of itself, and could only look about, there was so much to be seen. The court was close to a garden, where everything looked blooming. Fresh and fragrant roses hung over the little palings. The linden-trees were in blossom; while the swallows flew here and there, crying, "Twit, twit, twit, my mate is coming," but it was not the fir-tree they meant. "Now I shall live," cried the tree, joyfully spreading out its branches; but alas! they were all withered and yellow, and it lay in a corner amongst weeds and nettles. The star of gold paper still stuck in the top of the tree and glittered in the sunshine. In the same courtyard, two of the merry children were playing who had danced round the tree at Christmas and had been so happy. The youngest saw the gilded star and ran and pulled it off the tree.

"Look what is sticking to the ugly old fir-tree," said the child, treading on the branches till they crackled under his boots. And the tree saw all the fresh bright flowers in the garden, and then looked at itself, and wished it had remained in the dark corner of the garret. It thought of its fresh youth in the forest, of the merry Christmas evening, and of the little mice who had listened to the story of "Humpty Dumpty."

"Past! past!" said the old tree; "Oh, had I but enjoyed myself while I could have done so! But now it is too late." Then a lad came and chopped the tree into small pieces, till a large bundle lay in a heap on the ground. The pieces were placed in a fire under the copper, and they quickly blazed up brightly, while the tree sighed so deeply that each sigh was like a pistol-shot.

Then the children, who were at play, came and seated themselves in front of the fire, and looked at it and cried, "Pop, pop." But at each "pop," which was a deep sigh, the tree was thinking of a summer day in the forest; and of Christmas evening, and of "Humpty Dumpty," the only story it had ever heard or knew how to relate, till at last it was consumed. The boys still played in the garden, and the youngest wore the golden star on his breast, with which the tree had been adorned during the happiest evening of its existence.

Now all was past; the tree's life was past, and the story also,- for all stories must come to an end at last.

Fables

What are Fables?

Fables are a beautiful way to teach your child about morals, life lessons, and impart the wisdom of the ages in an engaging manner. Fables are stories that have been told throughout past generations, trickling down to the present to deliver important lessons about life, nature, love, friendship, and being a good person. More often than not a fable involves one or more animals who can speak and relate to your child. These characters are usually involved in some sort of moral conundrum or faced with a unique challenge that activates a child's creativity. This excites their imaginations and brings the necessary knowledge in a comforting way. Fables are deeply philosophical but simple enough for even the younger ones to grasp.

Positive Impacts

Through reading fables with your child you will be imparting truths to them that would otherwise be not so fun to teach. Each time you open up a book of fables your child will learn how to be brave in the face of adversity, how to cooperate with those close to them, how to accept everyone for who they are, and how to distinguish the wrong choice from the right one. These are effective tools that will stay with your child for their entire life because children are like little sponges. What you choose to read to them when they are still young can have an impact that is far-reaching. Children have consistently loved reading fables or having fables read to them, so do not be surprised when they ask for the fable book more than any others that they typically enjoy. Reading a fable is highly important in child development.

Benefits of Fables

The benefits of reading fables to a child are exponential. Your child will:

1. Become well-rounded morally
2. Learn important life lessons
3. Have a deeper connection with others
4. Your child will grow up having a more solid, rounded, and deeper moral foundation that will help shape his or her life choices as they grow up. The stories are memorable enough to where they will be able to recall at a moment's notice the imagery and situations presented in a classic fable. With this, they will understand how to handle different situations in life that would otherwise be

overwhelming or new. This will lead to better problem-solving skills, especially when the problem involves their feelings and the feelings of others. Your child will have more empathy for those who are different than they are. This is something that is perhaps most important because all through life he or she will have to interact with unique individuals. Fables instill a kind of empathy that may be hard to pass on in other ways.

Parents' Guidance

As a parent, it is simple to get started with fables. Simply find a book of popular fables, such as Aesop's Fables, and make it a habit to read a story twice a week to your child. There also exist plenty of online collections if you want to get started right away. It takes almost no time. If you would like to do something new, special, and time-honored, try reading a fable to your child. The effort is small, but the benefits are endless.

The Travelers and the Purse

Two men were traveling in a company along the road when one of them picked up a well-filled purse.

"How lucky I am!" he said. "I have found a purse. Judging by its weight it must be full of gold."

"Do not say 'I have found a purse,'" said his companion. "Say rather 'we have found a purse' and 'how lucky we are.' Travelers ought to share alike the fortunes or misfortunes of the road."

"No, no," replied the other angrily. "I found it and I am going to keep it."

Just then they heard a shout of "Stop, thief!" and looking around, saw a mob of people armed with clubs coming down the road.

The man who had found the purse fell into a panic.

"We are lost if they find the purse on us," he cried.

"No, no," replied the other, "You would not say 'we' before, so now stick to your 'I'. Say 'I am lost.'"

"We cannot expect anyone to share our misfortunes unless we are willing to share our good fortune also".

The Sheep and the Pig

One day a shepherd discovered a fat Pig in the meadow where his Sheep were pastured. He very quickly captured the porker, which squealed at the top of its voice the moment the Shepherd laid his hands on it. You would have thought, to hear the loud squealing, that the Pig was being cruelly hurt. But in spite of its squeals and struggles to escape, the Shepherd tucked his prize under his arm and started off to the butchers in the market place.

The Sheep in the pasture were much astonished and amused at the Pig's behavior and followed the Shepherd and his charge to the pasture gate.

"What makes you squeal like that?" asked one of the Sheep. "The Shepherd often catches and carries off one of us. But we should feel very much ashamed to make such a terrible fuss about it like you do."

"That is all very well," replied the Pig, with a squeal and a frantic kick. "When he catches you he is only after your wool. But he wants my bacon! gree-ee-ee!"

"It is easy to be brave when there is no danger".

The Farmer and the Stork

A Stork of a very simple and trusting nature had been asked by a gay party of Cranes to visit a field that had been newly planted. But the party ended dismally with all the birds entangled in the meshes of the Farmer's net.

The Stork begged the Farmer to spare him.

"Please let me go," he pleaded. "I belong to the Stork family who you know are honest and birds of good character. Besides, I did not know the Cranes were going to steal."

"You may be a very good bird," answered the Farmer, "but I caught you with the thieving Cranes and you will have to share the same punishment with them."

"You are judged by the company you keep".

The Plane Tree

Two Travellers, walking in the noonday sun, sought the shade of a wide-spreading tree to rest. As they lay looking up among the pleasant leaves, they saw that it was a Plane Tree.

"How useless is the Plane!" said one of them. "It bears no fruit whatever, and only serves to litter the ground with leaves."

"Ungrateful creatures!" said a voice from the Plane Tree. "You lie here in my cooling shade, and yet you say I am useless! Thus ungratefully, O Jupiter, do men receive their blessings!"

"Our best blessings are often the least appreciated".

The Gnat and the Bull

A gnat flew over the meadow with much buzzing for so small a creature and settled on the tip of one of the horns of a Bull. After he had rested a short time, he made ready to fly away. But before he left he begged the Bull's pardon for having used his horn for a resting place.

"You must be very glad to have me go now," he said.

"It's all the same to me," replied the Bull. "I did not even know you were there."

We are often of greater importance in our own eyes than in the eyes of our neighbor.

"The smaller the mind the greater the conceit".

The Lion and the Mouse

A Lion lay asleep in the forest, his great head resting on his paws. A timid little Mouse came upon him unexpectedly, and in her fright and haste to get away, ran across the Lion's nose. Roused from his nap, the Lion laid his huge paw angrily on the tiny creature to kill her.

"Spare me!" begged the poor Mouse. "Please let me go and someday I will surely repay you."

The Lion was much amused to think that a Mouse could ever help him. But he was generous and finally let the Mouse go.

Some days later, while stalking his prey in the forest, the Lion was caught in the toils of a hunter's net. Unable to free himself, he filled the forest with his angry roaring. The Mouse knew the voice and quickly found the Lion struggling in the net. Running to one of the great ropes that bound him, she gnawed it until it parted, and soon the Lion was free.

"You laughed when I said I would repay you," said the Mouse. "Now you see that even a Mouse can help a Lion."

"Kindness is never wasted".

The Ass and His Driver

An Ass was being driven along a road leading down the mountainside when he suddenly took it into his silly head to choose his own path. He could see his stall at the foot of the mountain, and to him, the quickest way down seemed to be over the edge of the nearest cliff. Just as he was about to leap over, his master caught him by the tail and tried to pull him back, but the stubborn Ass would not yield and pulled with all his might.

"Very well," said his master, "go your way, you willful beast, and see where it leads you."

With that, he let go, and the foolish Ass tumbled head over heels down the mountainside.

"They who will not listen to reason but stubbornly go their own way against the friendly advice of those who are wiser than they are on the road to misfortune".

The Wolf and the Crane

A Wolf had been feasting too greedily, and a bone had stuck crosswise in his throat. He could get it neither up nor down, and of course, he could not eat a thing. Naturally, that was an awful state of affairs for a greedy Wolf.

So away he hurried to the Crane. He was sure that she, with her long neck and bill, would easily be able to reach the bone and pull it out.

"I will reward you very handsomely," said the Wolf, "if you pull that bone out for me."

The Crane, as you can imagine, was very uneasy about putting her head in a Wolf's throat. But she was grasping in nature, so she did what the Wolf asked her to do.

When the Wolf felt that the bone was gone, he started to walk away.

"But what about my reward!" called the Crane anxiously.

"What!" snarled the Wolf, whirling around. "Haven't you got it? Isn't it enough that I let you take your head out of my mouth without snapping it off?"

"Expect no reward for serving the wicked".

The Fox and the Grapes

A Fox one day spied a beautiful bunch of ripe grapes hanging from a vine trained along the branches of a tree. The grapes seemed ready to burst with juice, and the Fox's mouth watered as he gazed longingly at them.

The bunch hung from a high branch, and the Fox had to jump for it. The first time he jumped he missed it by a long way. So he walked off a short distance and took a running leap at it, only to fall short once more. Again and again, he tried but in vain.

Now he sat down and looked at the grapes in disgust. "What a fool I am," he said. "Here I am wearing myself out to get a bunch of sour grapes that are not worth gaping for." And off he walked very, very scornfully.

"There are many who pretend to despise and belittle that which is beyond their reach".

The Kid and the Wolf

A frisky young Kid had been left by the herdsman on the thatched roof of a sheep shelter to keep him out of harm's way. The Kid was browsing near the edge of the roof, when he spied a Wolf and began to jeer at him, making faces and abusing him to his heart's content.
"I hear you," said the Wolf, "and I haven't the least grudge against you for what you say or do. When you are up there it is the roof that's talking, not you."

"Do not say anything at any time that you would not say at all times".

The Eagle and the Jackdaw

The Shepherd saw the fluttering Jackdaw and at once guessed what had happened. Running up, he caught the bird and clipped its wings. That evening he gave the Jackdaw to his children.

"What a funny bird this is!" they said laughing, "what do you call it, father?"

"That is a Jackdaw, my children. But if you should ask him, he would say he is an Eagle."

"Do not let your vanity make you overestimate your powers".

Section 1: TOM AND TALKING MOUSE

THE MILLER'S MOUSE

The reason why everyone loved Tom Lecky so much was, I believe that he was so good-tempered, so cheerful and so unselfish.

Tom was not good-looking, and, indeed, if one were disposed to be critical in such matters, one could have found fault with almost all his features except his eyes. These were brown like sealskin, and nearly always brimming over with merriment. But no one ever thought of criticizing Tom's features, and there was a common belief among the villagers that Tom was a handsome fellow. And indeed he was, for his beautiful, unselfish soul gave to his face a beauty which merely regular features can never do.

Tom Lecky owned a flour-mill, which was situated a little way from Ellingford, the village where he had been born. He was "well-off," for the mill brought him a good deal of money. He had no relations but hoped to have a very near one—a wife. This was Anne Grey, the blacksmith's daughter, who was as pretty as she was winsome. She was fond of pretty things too, flowers especially, so it was Tom's delight to gratify her fancy.

For this reason, he bought Brooks's cottage, which had a lovely garden. And week by week he purchased this or that to make his cottage pretty and home-like for his bride. It would be difficult to tell how much pleasure Tom found in furnishing this cottage. He would wander in the garden-paths among the rose-bushes, smiling to himself as he thought of the many surprises in store for Anne. But a surprise was in store for him which was not at all pleasant. Anne Grey married someone else.

When Tom heard it, he locked up the pretty cottage, put the key in his pocket, and went to the mill to live. To Anne, he spoke no word, though he saw her with her husband coming from the church. He spoke to no one but did his work at the mill like a man in a dream. Some there were who tried to break through his stony reserve, but no one succeeded. Tom Lecky had become hard and soured. He remained alone in the mill—except for the mice, and these, he set traps. He caught a great many, and plunged them, trap and all, into a bucket of water. When he found a trap with a mouse in it, he would look at the little creature beating itself against its prison, turning rapidly round, forcing its pointed nose between the wire bars, while its long tail was hanging down through the bars on the other side. He would watch the bright little eyes almost start from their sockets in fear and agony, and yet no feeling of sorrow or pity came into his heart for the tiny captive, and after a time with a smile on his face, he would drown the little creature. Could this be the Tom Lecky who had had almost the tenderness of a woman at the sight of pain?

Tom's "living-room" was in the basement of the mill. In it were a table, a chair, a bed, and a cupboard. There was also a hanging bookshelf, with a row of books on it, which Tom never opened now. Through the ceiling of this room descended a ladder white with flour. If you climbed this ladder, you found yourself in a room smothered with flour-dust, and your ears were almost deafened by the sound of the machinery overhead which the wind-impelled mill-wheel kept in motion, while the descending stream of ground floor traveled unceasingly down from the grinding-wheel to the bin below. There was a ladder from this room to the one above where the machinery was. There was also a room over this from which you could get outside and regulate the small spiny-looking wheel at the top to gain all the force of the wind. All these rooms were festooned with cobwebs quite white with flour. The spiders were white, too, which made them look larger. Even the mice caught in the traps were white with flour.

Now at eight o'clock every evening Tom sat down at the round wooden table and ate his bread and cheese by the light of a tallow candle inserted in the neck of a bottle. And every night at this time there crept out from a crevice near the cupboard a tiny brown mouse, covered with flour-dust. This little mouse seemed eager and hungry, but it never ventured near the traps where the alluring cheese smelt so deliciously. It would wait for Tom to drop a crumb, and then would dart after it and frisk away into its hole, to return and watch again for another crumb. This happened night after night until Tom began to watch for the little creature with some eagerness. The sound of its tiny scampering feet on the floor would call up a feeling of pleasure like that which one feels when the knock of a dear friend is heard on the door. But Tom was bitter for all this, and at times he had a savage hope that the little mouse would, after all, be lured into one of the traps. He did not want to feel tender or kindly any more to anything. He tried to feel cruel and heartless because his tenderness had cost him so much pain.

Little girls with flowers

One autumn evening, when the air was still, and a sweet afterglow rested on the sky like an echo of the sunset, Tom sat thinking in his chair. It was then that he saw something which he never forgot. He saw his small friend watching one of the traps in which another mouse had just been caught. "Now it will shun me," thought Tom. "It has seen what the traps are for." But the tiny brown creature did not run away, as might have been expected, but crept up to the miller as trustfully as ever; indeed, more so, for it came upon the table and nibbled at a piece of bread close to Tom's hand. Then Tom arose, and went towards the trap, and, instead of drowning the captive, opened the door and set it at liberty. From that time he set no more traps. And he fell to thinking with shame that he had not given even a "Good-day" to those who had brought their corn to him to grind, and that when he passed through the village he had spurned children and dogs who had once been favorites of his, and had come to him with the confidence of old playmates. He remembered that some he had known and cared for had passed through sickness and trouble, and he had not gone to cheer them with a single word. And all this because he was unhappy.

And as he pondered with ever-increasing shame, the mouse crept up again and nibbled at his bread. "In spite of what this mouse has seen, it can still trust me," he thought, "and I, because one deceived me, have mistrusted all the world!"

Then he got up and put on his hat, and went out into the twilight. A little breeze had sprung up, and the trees seemed to be whispering together. He seemed to know what they said, though he could not have put it into words. He felt as if his old happiest self were rising once more from the tomb in which his resentment had buried it. It was not the light-hearted self which had once been, but it was the old loving, unselfish Tom for all that. He wandered on aimlessly at first, but afterward with definite intentions. He would go to Brooks's cottage. He could bear to do so now. He would see how the neglected garden had done without him, and perhaps to-morrow put it to rights.

When Tom reached the garden gate (it was a tall wicket-gate through which you could get a peep at the garden), he undid the padlock, and in the half-light saw a tall holly-hock stretching itself across the entrance as if barring the way. "The garden is ours—mine and the rest of the flowers," it seemed to say. "Why do you come to disturb our peace?—you who have forsaken us."

And the miller's heart answered, "If one who has forsaken you should come back, would you not receive him?" And then there came into his mind a glad though. Anne Grey might someday turn to him in trouble, and then he would help her, and never—certainly never—blame her. This thought warmed his heart as he passed into the garden. How sweet was the breath of the flowers! How their delicate shapes outlined themselves in the twilight! There was the little arbor over which Tom had trained the honeysuckle and blush-roses. He had often fancied Anne sitting there in the long summer afternoons sewing and singing to herself. Now the trailers of the rose half hid the entrance, and a bat flew out at the sound of Tom's step. Night moths flitted hither and thither, and winged beetles made the air vibrate with their drowsy buzzing. The stars began to peep out one after another, and a hush seemed to fall on the garden as if the flowers were asleep.

Then Tom stooped his tall form under the rose-trailers and entered the arbor. There was a table in it, and a sort of fixture-seat all round. Tom had made it himself at leisure moments. "If we have little ones," he had said to himself, "there will be a seat for them all." Now he sat in the arbor alone, and the rose-trailers moved in and out with a rustling sound.

The sounds and scents made Tom quite tired, and he presently imagined he saw and heard things which never could have happened. But they were so beautiful that he liked to think them real even afterward.

The table in the center of the arbor was fixed, and upon it, Tom leaned his arms. So he could see the glimmer of the sky between the branches, and one single bright star that looked, as he thought, kindly on him. He gazed and gazed at the star, and at the outlined branches, and the peep of the sky, till all his heart seemed to open to good—and that is to God. He gazed till self was forgotten in a beautiful dream. Ah! Happiness, he saw, did not consist in self-gratification, but in giving up for others. Then he closed his eyes like a child who has wept but is comforted, and it was then that he heard the little brown mouse talking with the flowers. Now the mouse was at the mill, as we know, so this was very odd.

Tom dreaming

" Why is the miller so sad?" asked a tall lily.

"First of all," said the mouse, "because Anne Grey is married to someone else, but most of all because he has made so many others bear his sorrow."

"And did making others bear his sorrow make his painless?" the sunflower asked.

"No," said the mouse, "it made it more; for he had to feel cruel as well as unhappy."

Then a tiny late Linum-flower spoke.

"I have not lived a long while," said the Linum-flower; "I came out late. I don't quite understand it, but I think it must be best to wait for one's joy. It may be the miller is to have more joy because he has to wait."

Then a yew-tree spoke.

"You are right, little Linum-flower; my relations in the graveyard have told me as much. They hear what the dead say at midnight. It is those who wait who get the truest joy!"

Then the miller heard a voice which was not like the others. It was a baby-voice with tears in it. "I am hungry," it said; and Tom started up, his eyes wide open, and in the star-glimmer, he saw a tiny child looking at him. Yes, he was awake, and the child was a real child.

"I came in here," said the little one "because the gate was open."

The miller took the little one in his arms and kissed it.

"So you are hungry," he said caressingly. "Well, I must take you home. What is your name?"

"Dot," said the child; "and home is gone away on wheels, and uncle doesn't want me no more."

"Uncle," repeated Tom reflectively. "Then have you no mother or father, little one?"

"Never had none of these things," said Dot positively. "Some of the other children had, though," she added, as if for the sake of accuracy.

"What other children?" Tom asked with interest.

"Them as was with us in the van," said Dot.

"Did you live in a van, Dot?" inquired Tom.

"Yes," said the child, "the van as has run away. There are baskets and chairs and things all over the top of it. Uncle said he was going to leave me somewhere, and now he's done it."

"How old are you, Dot?"

The child shook her head. "I didn't have no birfdays," she said wistfully. "Ned and Polly and Jim did, but not me."

"Little Dot," cried Tom, hugging the small creature, "so they wanted to get rid of you, did they! Well, you shall come home with me; and, Dot, you shall begin to have birthdays to-morrow!"

"And some bread and dripping to-night—all across the loaf?" Dot asked anxiously.

"Yes, Dot, lots of times across the loaf if you want it."

"I will sell feather brushes for you," said Dot with enthusiasm.

Tom laughed. He had never laughed before all the summer through.

When Tom and Dot reached the mill, it was quite dark, and Dot had to stand still in the doorway while the miller lit his candle. When the candle was lit, the first thing Dot saw was the little brown mouse scudding across the table. She clapped her hands with delight, for she was not a bit afraid of mice. But the noise she made frightened the mouse, and it ran into its hole and never came out again all that night.

Mouse at mouse-hole

Tom slept on a heap of flour bags, for you see he had tucked Dot up snugly in his bed; but he slept soundly and well, for it is not so much the kind of bed we lie on, as the thoughts we lie down with, that give us pleasant sleep, and of all thoughts the best is that of having done some good and unselfish action in the day.

Dot proved uncommonly useful next morning. Tiny creature though she was, she was quite learned in domestic affairs. She lit the fire and tidied up the room before Tom was even awake. Indeed, when he did wake, it was to see her perched on his chair peeping into the cupboard to find the breakfast service. Tom's breakfast service was not extensive. It consisted of a huge cup and saucer a good deal chipped, two plates and a jam pot, this last article doing duty as a sugar-basin.

Dot was well used to make-shifts, for she even invented a new one. Upon the mantelshelf was a curious old vase with a griffin's head surrounding it. It was shaped like a jug, so

Dot took it down and washed it, saying to herself, "This will make a fine milk-jug."

"A fine milk-jug?" yawned the miller from his flour-bag couch. "Ah, to be sure! children want the milk to drink." And with this, he threw on his clothes, and hastily washed in a water-butt which stood near the mill steps. Then he called to Dot. "Come, little one, bring your milk-jug; we will go to the farm for milk for your breakfast."

"But we want to fetch the milk in a can," objected Dot.

Tom stunningly scratched his head for a moment; then, a happy thought struck him. "My beer-can will do, won't it?" he asked.

"Yes," answered Dot thoughtfully, "only first, it must be scrubbed."

So Tom scrubbed the can obediently, and when it shone sufficiently the two started off to a neighboring farm to buy the milk.

On the way from the farm, a strange thing happened. Tom and Dot were trudging merrily along a little lane, when they perceived a woman crouching under a hedge, holding in her arms a bundle wrapped in a shawl. The woman might have escaped notice, perhaps, had not a cry proceeded from the bundle. Tom had of late heard so many cries in his heart that his ear readily lent itself to one from outside. He came up to the woman, therefore, at once and said, "You have a little one wrapped in that, haven't you? Is it hungry? If it is, here is some milk."

At first, the woman did not raise her head. It was hidden in the shawl which covered the infant, so the miller repeated his question. Then the woman looked up, and the eyes which met Tom's were those of Anne Grey. She knew Tom at once, but it was with no smile of pleasure that she greeted him. Her words, too, when they came, were hard and cold. She only said, "So, Tom Lecky, you see what I have come to; rejoice in it!"

"Does the little one want food?" Tom asked again without noticing in any way the words or the tone of the woman.

"And if it does?" said Anne, with a bitter little laugh.

"Why, if it does, I'm ready to give it some," said Tom, passing his coat-sleeve before his eyes for a moment. Then removing it suddenly he smiled into the woman's face—an April sort of smile, which scarcely knows whether to cloud over or to beam out with full warmth—and said, "And if you want anything I can give, it is yours for the taking."

The woman burst into tears, and the child, which was scarcely more than a baby, cried to bear her company. It was then that little Dot came forward and took the shawled bundle in her baby arms, and commenced to feed it from the milk-can.

"How is it you are so early?" inquired Tom anxiously, for he knew that Anne's new home was many miles away.

"I have been here all night," she made answer.

"Anne, the cottage is still there, and the bit of furniture in it; go there, Anne—go now."

So Anne went after all to the cottage, which had been so long prepared for her, but it was not with Tom. He stayed at the mill with little Dot. And every night, when the child lay sleeping, the brown mouse crept out to bear the miller company. It was about this time that Tom thought the mouse began to talk to him as it had talked with the flowers in the garden the night he had found Dot.

"Miller," said the mouse, "is it not small things which make one happy?"

"Some things may content one, but it takes great ones to make one happy," said he.

"Contentment is happiness," said the mouse.

Now while the mouse was speaking, the candle, which was, as we have said, in the neck of a bottle instead of a candlestick, went out and dropped right to the bottom of the bottle. There was a tiny spark seen for some time through the green glass, and by its light, the miller saw many strange things, and the mouse was mixed up with them all.

The first thing he saw was a misty little ladder, made apparently of the cobwebs which festooned the mill. The ladder reached from the table right up through the floor and through the next floor, and from thence right up through the roof. A star was seen gleaming on its top. Up to this strange ladder, the little mouse ran, and the miller saw it by the light of the tiny spark, which somehow shot out upward rays which lit the ladder from top to bottom. When the mouse reached the top, a tiny creature floated down from the star and presented it with a gift. This the mouse brought down and laid on the table before the miller. At first, he thought it was sparked from the candle, but as he looked closer, he found they formed glittering words, but they were in a language he could not read.

Mouse at cobweb ladder

"What is the language?" he asked the mouse.

"The language of the eyes," answered the mouse.

"Read it to me," said the miller.

And the mouse read: "Tom, I am sorry—I am lonely; my husband and parents are dead. Tom, have you forgotten the old days?"

"It must be Anne's eyes which say this," cried the miller. "Yes, I might have read it all along."

Then the filmy ladder disappeared, and in the green light rose the little garden where the spring flowers were growing now. Within the arbor where Tom had gone to sleep one night sat Anne, her hands engaged in knitting, her eyes looking far away.

"Mouse, what is she thinking?" asked the miller. "You seem to know everything."

"Her eyes are talking," said the mouse.

"And what do they say?"

"They say, 'The miller only pities me; he no longer loves me.'"

"Ah, the eyes are wrong," cried Tom. "I will go to her and tell her so."

"Not yet," said the mouse. "Wait."

And then among the flowers there appeared a little child, and the child spoke low to the flowers.

"Listen," said the mouse.

"Oh, flowers, I have no father," murmured the child.

"Stop," cried the miller, "I must go."

And as he said this, the light went quite out, and in the dim starlight which shone through the window, he saw the mouse nibbling a crust of bread near his elbow. But for this little rustling sound, and Dot's breathing, all was silent. There were voices in the miller's heart, which made themselves heard well enough. One was the voice of Hope, the other the voice of Love.

So next day, when the sun was setting, Tom put on his best clothes, and, taking Dot by the hand, walked towards Brooks's cottage. When they reached it, Anne's little child stood in the gateway.

"Little one," said Tom, stooping and kissing the child, "his a mother in the garden?"

The child pointed to the arbor.

"Stay together, children," said the miller; and then he entered the arbor.

"What did I tell you?" said the mouse. The miller was in the old room at the mill for the last night.

"It matters little what you told me," said the miller—"you taught me so much."

Now from this time the mouse spoke no more to Tom, though he often saw the little brown creature. It is only to the lonely and sorrowful that mice and trees and clouds and wind talk much. And the miller was happy, for had not

Anne consented to marry him, and was not the wedding-day no farther distant now than to-morrow?

Anne visited the mill with her husband a week later, and she said, "There are many mice here. Why don't you set traps for them?"

"I cannot do that," said the miller. "One mouse has taught me more than all the books I have read. The mice are welcome to what they take of the grain."

And Anne questioned no more. It was enough for her that she and Tom were together. So I suppose the little brown mouse, or at least its descendants, still live on unmolested at the mill.

THE MESSAGE OF THE LILY

"Little flower, little flower," said the birdie, "why are you so silent and sad?"

"I am not sad, sweet sister," whispered the flower gently; "ah! No, but I have seen an angel. Yestreen, as I slept, my birdie, being all aweary with gazing up into your bird-land home among the branches and watching the merry sunlight come and go, and strike shafts of golden flame among the green, I dreamt of heaven and the holy angels; and lo! when I awoke, one there was who stood beside me, beautiful even as is the sunlight or the dawn, and her voice, when she spoke, was low and tender, like the restful ripple of the rain. And to the flowers, as you know, my birdie, the hearts of the pure lie ever open and unsealed, and I saw into her heart, that the thought of it was white and spotless as a lily, and I saw that he thought was a prayer, and that she said, 'Dear Lord, I thank Thee for making this little flower so fair and lovely, and I ask Thee that I may be, in heart, as pure and holy as she!'"

MORNING

"Wake up, little flower, and hear what I have to tell you," said the bird gaily, "for I, too, have seen your angel—and the angel is she none, but the fairest maiden from the town beyond the hillside."

And to her, the flower made low reply:

"Can anyone as fair as she is found out of heaven? And, moreover, I looked into her heart, and saw that the thought of it was white and pure as the morning."

Little Girls Picking Flowers

"It is only the flowers that can see into hearts," said the bird gravely; "but this I know, that your angel is of earth, not heaven." So saying, she spread her silken wings and flew away.

But the flower said, "Is there, in all heaven, anything fairer than a maiden?"

NOON

"I would not pluck you to please my idle fancies, dear blossom," said the maiden gently, "for I cannot bear to see the wildflowers wither and fade! But I know of one who lies ill and dying, to whom the scent and sight of a wildflower may bring some passing moment of peace. Tell me, then, you who are so pure and lovely, will not you spare space of your slender life, that so you may make happy the heart of a sorrowing one?"

Then the flower said, "Dear maiden, I will"; but since it spake not the maiden's language, it breathed forth all its perfume, like sweet music, in consent. And, though the maiden knew not that the flower had heard her words, and had answered her, yet at heart, she was strange though sweetly saddened. "Even in heaven I should long for the earth-flowers!" she said, as she drank in the fragrance. "Is there anything, in all heaven, fairer than a flower?"

Then the maiden plucked the flower, and bore it away from the birds and the sunshine, away from the wind and the trees, to a squalid court in a great city, where a dying woman lay, haggard and wan, upon a bed. And as the flower looked into the soul of the dying woman, its fair leaves seemed to wither and wilt, as though some foul breath had come forth upon it, for therein it could see nothing because of the blackness and the sin. And at first the flower shrank into itself, and would fain have gathered up its perfume, but it thought of the prayer in the maiden's heart, and, opening out its snowy petals to their full, it breathed forth a fragrance which filled the foul room as with music and light. And as the dying woman looked upon the flower, she thought of the white lilies which she had gathered and placed upon her dead mother's bosom— many, ah! So many weary years ago; and she thought of the days when she too was pure and beautiful and had knelt at that mother's knee, to whisper, after her, the hallowed words to the Father in heaven.

Then the flower saw that in the woman's heart, there was some strange and sudden commotion, as though the light were seeking to win in its way and to drive out the darkness and sin.

And, folding her wasted hands together, the dying woman turned to the light, and said, "Dear Lord Jesus, make me—even me—white and pure as this lily, and wash away all my sins in Thy precious blood. Amen."

And when the dawn came, the flower lay withered and drooping; but, ere it died, it saw into the woman's heart that it was white and pure as the snow-flake.

And there passed from that room a shining angel, and lo! on her bosom lay a little flower.

WATER-LILY'S MISSION

"Come away, beautiful flower," said the kingfisher; "do not waste your beauty in this melancholy mere; float away down the gleaming river where tall bulrushes grow and where you shall find companions."

But the water-lily said, "No, I cannot go, for up in yonder tower is a prisoner, and I cheer his lonely days. He watches me and smiles, and forgets that he is a captive. I cannot leave one so unhappy."

"As you like," said the kingfisher, "but you would not catch me spending my life under those barren walls," and away flew the kingfisher.

A swallow came and wheeled round and round the tower. "Swallow," called the water-lily, "come to me." And the swallow came twittering down.

"I am in a great hurry," he said; "what do you want?"

"Bite through my stem, swallow, and carry me up to the grating in the tower, and place me on that window-sill."

"But you will die—and you are so beautiful," said the swallow, looking regretfully at the lily.

"Ah, some deaths are better than living," said the water-lily.

So the swallow plucked the water-lily and carried her up to the prisoner's window. A thin hand passed through the bars and took the flower. The captive pressed her passionately to his lips, and his tears fell fast on the waxen petals as the tears fell, the water-lily revived.

"How beautiful you are," said the captive, and he took his tin mug of water from a shelf and tenderly placed her in it so she would not die.

Just then, a jailer entered, "Ho, ho!" he said, "how did you come by that; it will just do for my button-hole." And he seized the water-lily and placed it in his coat.

The poor prisoner fell upon his knees and begged hard that the flower might be left to him. "Let me have a few days' joy," he pleaded. "The flower will soon die, and you are free, and can gather the flowers when you will."

But the rough jailer only laughed, and departed to his pleasant room, leaving the captive in tears.

Child with a basket of flowers

"Look here," said the jailer to his little daughter, "there is a flower I have just taken away from the prisoner in the tower. I don't know how he got it, but he cried like a baby when I took it away."

"Poor prisoner!" said the little girl, with tears in her own eyes.

"Nay, my little maid, do not weep," said the jailer, taking the child in his arms.

But the little one hid her face against her father's breast and sobbed.

"See, my Lily, I will take his flower back to him, only do not cry so," said the jailer.

"Father, may I take it to him?" said the little girl, raising her tear-stained face to her father's, and gazing at him eagerly.

"Won't it do if I take it?" asked the jailer.

"Oh, please let me take it," said the child.

The rough jailer had such tenderness for his child that it was difficult for him to refuse her anything. So it was that when the prisoner lifted his weary head as he heard his door open, he beheld a beautiful child with blue eyes and yellow hair, and in her hand stretched out to him was the water-lily.

"Oh, but it is an angel!" cried the prisoner, a smile lighting his haggard face. "An angel from heaven; I must be going to die."

"No, poor man, it's little Lily," said the child, and she slid around arm about his neck. "I am so sorry for you!"

The prisoner burst into passionate weeping and kissed the small hand that lay upon his shoulder.

The jailer blew his nose like a trumpet.

"You may be called anything," said the prisoner, "but you are surely an angel."

From this time, Lily came to see her prisoner every day, and he grew almost gay.

In the meantime, the water-lily drooped and died, but she was happy, for she had fulfilled her mission.

The prisoner took the dead flower and laid it on his heart. "Poor little dead flower," he said, "it was you who brought me my little comforter."

As he said these words, he fancied he felt the dead flower move, but it might have been the beating of his own heart.

—

THE END

Section 2: JESSY

Once upon a time, there was a little girl named Jessy because she cried so often.

If she could not have her way, she cried; if she could not have everything for which she wished, she cried.

Her mother told her one day that she would melt away in tears if she cried so often. "You are like the boy who cried for the moon," she told her, "and if it had been given to him it would not have made him happy, for what possible use could the moon be to anyone out of its proper place? And that is the way with you; half the things for which you cry would be of no use to you if you got them."

Jessy did not take warning or heed her mother's words of wisdom and kept on crying just the same.

One morning she was crying as she walked along to school because she wanted to stay at home when she noticed a frog hopping along beside her.

"Why are you following me?" she asked, looking at him through her tears.

"Because you will soon form a pond around you with your tears," replied the frog, "and I have always wanted a pond all to myself."

"I shall not make any pond for you," said Jessy, "and I do not want you following me, either."

The frog continued to hop along beside her, and Jessy stopped crying and began to run, but the frog hopped faster, and she could not get away from him, so she began to cry again.

"Go away, you horrid green frog!" she said.

At last, she was so tired she sat on a stone by the roadside, crying all the time.

"Now," replied the frog, "I shall soon have my pond."

Jessy cried harder than ever, then; she could not see, her tears fell so fast, and by and by she heard a splashing sound. She opened her eyes and saw water all around her.

She was on a small island in the middle of the pond; the frog hopped out of the pond, making a terrible grimace as he sat down beside her.

"I hope you are satisfied," said Jessy. "You have your pond; why don't you stay in it?"

"Alas!" replied the frog, "I have wished for something which I cannot use now that I have it. Your tears are salt, and my pond, which I have all by myself is so salty that I cannot enjoy it. If only your tears had been fresh, I should have been a most fortunate fellow."

"You needn't stay if you do not like it," said Jessy, "and you needn't find fault with my tears, either," she said, beginning to cry again.

"Stop! stop!" cried the frog, hopping about excitedly; "you will have a flood if you keep on crying."

Jessy saw the water rising around her, so she stopped a minute. "What shall I do?" she asked. "I cannot swim, and I will die if I have to stay here," and then she began to cry again.

The frog hopped up and down in front of her, waving his front legs and telling her to hush. "If you would only stop crying," he said, "I might be able to help you, but I cannot do a thing if you cover me with your salt tears."

Jessy listened and promised she would not cry if he would get her away from the island.

"There is only one way that I know of," said the frog; "you must smile; that will dry the pond, and we can escape."

"But I do not feel like smiling," said Jessy, and her eyes filled with tears again.

"Look out!" said the frog; "you will surely be drowned in your tears if you cry again."

Jessy began to laugh. "That would be queer, wouldn't it, to be drowned in my tears?" she said.

"That is right, keep on smiling," said the frog; "the pond is smaller already." And he stood up on his hind legs and began to dance for joy.

Jessy laughed again. "Oh, you are so funny!" she said. "I wish I had your picture. I never saw a frog dance before."

"You have a slate under your arm," said the frog. "Why don't you draw a picture of me?" The frog picked up a stick and stuck it in the ground, and then he leaned on it with one arm, or front leg, and, crossing his feet, he stood very still.

Jessy drew him in that position, and then he kicked up his legs as if he were dancing, and she tried to draw him that way, but it was not a very good likeness.

"Do you like that?" she asked the frog when she held the slate for him to see. He looked so surprised that Jessy laughed again. "You did not think you were handsome, did you?" she asked.

"I had never thought I looked as bad as those pictures," replied the frog. "Let me try drawing your picture," he said.

"Now look pleasant," he said, as he seated himself in front of Jessy, "and do smile."

Jessy did as he requested, and in a few minutes, he handed her the slate. "Where is my nose?" asked Jessy, laughing.

"Oh, I forgot the nose!" said the frog. "But don't you think your eyes are nice and large, and your mouth, too?"

"They are certainly big in this picture," said Jessy. "I hope I do not look just like that."

"I do not think either of us as artists," replied the frog.

Jessy looked around her. "Why, where is the pond?" she asked. "It is gone."

"I thought it would dry up if you would only smile," said the frog; "and I think both of us have learned a lesson. I shall never again wish for a pond of my own. I should be lonely without my companions, and then, it might be salt, just as this one was. And you surely will never cry over little things again, for you see what might happen to you, and then you look so much prettier smiling."

"Perhaps I do," said Jessy, "but your pictures of me make me doubt it. However, I feel much happier smiling, and I do not want to be on an island again, even with such a pleasant companion as you were."

"Look out for the tears, then," said the frog as he hopped away.

THE END

Section 3: WHY THE MORNING-GLORY SLEEPS

One day the flowers got into a very angry discussion over the sun, of whom they were very fond.

"Surely, you all must know that he loves me best," said the rose. "He shines upon me and makes me sweeter than any of you, and he gives me the colors that are most admired by man."

"I do not see how you can say that," said the dahlia. "You may give forth more fragrance than I can, but you cannot think for a second that you are more beautiful why my colors are richer than yours and last much longer! The sun certainly loves me the best."

The modest lily looked at the dahlia and said in a low, sweet voice, "I do not wish to be bold, but I feel that the sun loves me and that I should let you know that he gives me more fragrance than to any of you."

"Oh, oh! Hear Lily!" said the others in chorus. "She thinks the king of day loves her best."

The lily hung her head and said no more, for the other flowers quite frightened her with their taunts.

"How can any of you think you are the best beloved of the sun?" said golden glow. "When you behold my glowing color which the sun bestows on me, do any of you look so much like him as I do? No, indeed; he loves me best."

The hollyhock looked down on the others with pitying glances. "It is plain to be seen that you have never noticed that the sun shines on me with more warmth than on you, and now I must tell you he loves me best and gives me the tenderest of his smiles. See how tall I am and how gorgeous are my colors. He loves me best."

"When it comes to sweetness, I am sure you have forgotten me," said the honeysuckle. "Why the king of the day loves me best, you may be sure! He makes me give forth more sweetness than any of you."

"You may be very sweet," said the pansy, "but surely you know that my pet name is heart's-ease and that the sun loves me best. To none of you does he give such velvet beauty as to me. I am nearest his heart and his best beloved."

The morning-glory listened to all this with envy in her heart. She did not give forth sweetness, as many of the others, neither did she possess the beauty of the rose or the pansy.

"If only I could get him to notice me," she thought. "I am dainty and frail, and I am sure he would admire me if only he could behold me, but the others are always here and in such glowing colors that their beauty overshadows poor little me."

All day morning-glory thought of the sun and wondered how she could attract his attention to herself, and at night she smiled, for she had thought of a plan. She would get up early in the morning and greet him before the other flowers were awake.

She went to bed early that night so that she might not oversleep in the morning, and when the first streak of dawn showed in the sky, morning-glory opened her eyes and shook out her delicate folds. The dew was on her, and she turned her face toward the sun.

As soon as she peeped into the garden, the sun beheld her. "How dainty and lovely you are!" he said. "I have never noticed before the beauty of your colors, morning-glory," and he let his warm glances fall and linger upon her.

The sunflower all this time was watching with jealous eyes, for she was the one who had always welcomed the sun, and this morning, he seemed to have entirely forgotten her.

Still, sunflower kept her gaze upon them and wondered what she could do to win back her kingdom from the delicate little morning-glory.

But as she looked, she saw the morning-glory sway and nod her head. "She is going to sleep," said the sunflower; "his warm breath makes her drowsy, or else she was up so early that she cannot keep awake."

While the sunflower watched, sure enough, the morning-glory nodded and closed her eyes. She was fast asleep, and the fickle sun, seeing that she no longer looked upon him, looked away and beheld the sunflower looking toward him with longing eyes.

"Good morning, King," she said, as she caught his eye, and she was wise enough not to let him know she had seen him before. So the sun smiled and turned his face upon them all, and the sunflower kept to herself what she had seen, knowing full well that she was the one who knew best how to keep his first and last glances.

A little later, one of the flowers called out: "Look at morning-glory; she is still sleeping. Let us tell her it is time to awaken."

"Morning-glory! morning-glory!" they called, but she did not answer. She was sound asleep.

"That is strange," said the rose. "I wonder if she has gone to sleep never to awake. I have heard of such things happening."

After two or three mornings, the other flowers ceased to notice morning-glory, for they thought she had ceased to be one of them, but the wise sunflower kept her own counsel. She knew that morning-glory had to sleep all day so that she might not miss the sun; but, as I told you, she was wise enough not to complain, and she kept his love for her by so doing.

THE END

Section 4: CHARITY AND THE PORTRAIT

Charity was very fond of her grandmother and grandfather and liked to visit them, but there were no little girls to play with, and sometimes she was lonely for someone her age. She would wander about the house looking for the queer things that grandmothers always have in their homes. The hall clock interested Charity very much. It stood on the landing at the top of the stairs, and she used to sit and listen to its queer tick-tock and watch the hands, which moved with little nervous jumps. Then there were on its face the stars and the moon and the sun, and they all were very wonderful to Charity. One day she went into the big parlor, where there were pictures of her grandfather and grandmother, and her great-grandfather and great-grandmother, also.

Charity thought the "greats" looked very sedate, and she felt sure they must have been very old to have been the parents of her grandfather. But the picture that interested her the most was a large painting of three children, one a little girl about her age, and one other older, and a boy, who wore queer-looking trousers, cut off below the knee. His suit was of black velvet, and he wore white stockings and black shoes. The little girls were dressed in white, and their dresses had short sleeves and low necks. The older girl had black hair, but the one that Charity thought was her age had long, golden curls like hers, only the girl in the picture wore her hair parted, and the curls hung all about her face.

Charity climbed into a big chair and sat looking at them. "I wish they could play with me," she thought, and she smiled at the little golden-haired girl. And then, wonderful to tell, the girl in the picture smiled at Charity.

"Oh! are you alive?" asked Charity.

"Of course I am," the little girl replied. "I will come down if you would like to have me, and visit with you."

"Oh, I should be so glad to have you!" Charity answered.

Then the boy stepped to the edge of the frame, and from there to the top of a big chair which stood under the picture, and stood in the chair seat. He held out his hand to the little girls and helped them to the floor in the most courtly manner. Charity got out of her chair and asked them to be seated, and the boy placed chairs for them beside her.

"What is your name?" asked the golden-haired girl, for she was the only one who spoke.

"That was my name," she said when Charity told her. "I lived in this house," she continued, "and we used to have such good times. This is my sister and my brother." The little girl and boy smiled, but they let their sister do all the talking. "We used to roast chestnuts in the fireplace," she said, "and once we had a party in this room, and played all sorts of games."

Charity could not imagine that a quiet room filled with children.

"Do you remember how we frightened poor old Uncle Zack in this room?" she said to her brother and sister, and then they all laughed.

"Do tell me about it," said Charity.

"These glass doors by the fireplace did not have curtains in our day," said the little girl, "and there were shells and other things from the ocean in one cupboard, and in the other, there were a sword and a helmet and a pair of gauntlets. My brother wrapped a sheet around him and put on the helmet and the gauntlets, and, taking the sword in his hand, he climbed into the cupboard and sat down. We girls closed the doors and hid behind the sofa. Uncle Zack came in to fix the fire, and my brother beckoned to him. Poor Zack dropped the wood he was carrying and fell on his knees, trembling with fright. The door was not fastened, and my brother pushed it open and pointed the sword at poor Uncle Zack.

"'Don' hurt a po' ol' nigger,' said Zack, very faintly. 'I 'ain' don' noffin,' 'deed I 'ain."

"'You told about the jam the children ate,' said my brother, in a deep voice, 'and you know you drank the last drop of rum Mammy Sue had for her rheumatism, and for this you must be punished,' and he brought the sword down on the floor of the cupboard with a bang.

"Poor Uncle Zack fell on his face with fright. This was too much for my sister and me, and we laughed out.

"You never saw anyone change so quickly as Uncle Zack. He jumped up, and we ran, but my brother had to get out of his disguise, and Uncle Zack caught him. He agreed not to tell our father if we did not tell about his fright, and so we escaped being punished."

"Tell me more about your life in this old house," said Charity, when the little girl finished her story. But just then the picture of Charity's great-grandmother moved and out she stepped from her frame. She walked with a very stately air toward the children and put her hand on the shoulder of the little girl who had been telling the story, and said: "You better go back to your frame now."

"Oh, dear!" said the little girl. "I did so dislike being grown up, and I had forgotten all about it when my grown-up self-reminds me. That is the trouble when you are in the room with your grown-up picture," she told Charity. "You see, I had to be so sedated after I married that I never even dared to think of my girlhood, but you come in here again someday, and I will tell you more about the good times we had."

The boy mounted the chair first and helped his sisters back into the frame. Charity looked for her great-grandmother, but she, too, was back in her frame, looking as sedate as ever. The next day Charity asked her grandmother who the children were in the big picture.

"This one," she said, pointing to the little golden-haired girl, "was your great-grandmother; you were named for her, and the other little girl and boy were your grandfather's aunt and uncle. They were your great-great-aunt and uncle."

Charity did not quite understand the "great-great" part of it, but she was glad to know that her stately-looking great-grandmother had once been a little girl like her, and someday, when the great-grandmother's picture is not looking, she expects to hear more about the fun the children had in the days long ago.

THE END

Section 5: JOE

Joe was one of those little boys who seemed to have grown up on the streets of the big city where he lived.

He never remembered a mother or a father, and no one ever took care of him. His first remembrance was of an older woman who gave him a crust of bread, and he slept in the corner of her room. One day they carried her away, and since then Joe had slept in a doorway or an alley.

By selling papers, he managed to get enough to eat, and if he did not have the money, he stole to satisfy his hunger.

He was often cold and hungry, but he saw many other children that were in the same condition, and he did not suppose that anyone ever had enough to eat or a warm place to sleep every night.

Joe went into the Salvation Army meetings when they held them in his neighborhood because it was a place where the wind did not blow, and while there he heard them sing and talk about Some One who loved everybody and would help you if only you would ask Him. Joe was never able to find out just where this Person lived, and, therefore, he could not ask for help.

One day Joe saw a lady who was too well dressed to belong in his part of the city, and he followed her, thinking that she might have a pocket-book he could take. The opportunity did not offer itself, however, and before Joe realized it, he was in a part of the city he had never seen before.

The buildings were tall and the streets much cleaner than where he lived. Joe walked along, looking in windows of the stores when he noticed a lady standing beside him with a jeweled watch hanging from her belt.

He had never seen anything so beautiful or so easy to take, and he waited for a few more people to gather around the window, and then he carefully reached for the watch, and with one pull off came the trinket, and away ran Joe, like a deer, with the watch clasped firmly in his begrimed little hand.

On and on he ran, not knowing where he was going-- nor caring, for that matter--and it seemed to Joe that the whole world was crying, "Stop, thief!" and was chasing him.

After a while, the noise grew fainter and fainter, and he stopped and looked back. There was not a person in sight.

Joe looked around him. All the houses were large with clean stone steps in front of them. Joe sat down on the bottom step of one of these houses and looked at his treasure.

He held it to his ear and heard its soft tick; then he looked at the sparkling stones on the case. He opened it and watched the little hands move, then he opened the back part, and there was the picture of a baby, a little boy, Joe thought. Around its chubby face were curled, and its eyes were large and earnest-looking. Joe sat gazing at it for some minutes, wondering who it was. When he looked up, he saw a large building across the street with a steeple on it, and on the top of that across.

The door of the building was open, and after a while, Joe walked across the street and up the long, wide steps. He went in and looked cautiously about. It was still, and no one was to be seen.

There were two doors, and Joe went to one of them and pushed it open. He thought for a minute he was dreaming, for he did not suppose that anything so grand could be real.

There were rows and rows of seats, and at the very end of the big room, Joe saw a light. He walked down one of the aisles to where the little flame was burning and stood in front of the altar.

Joe looked at everything with a feeling of awe, but he had not the slightest idea of what it all meant, and he wondered who lived in this beautiful house and thought it strange that no one appeared and told him to go out.

There were pictures on the wall, and Joe came to one of a sweet-faced lady who was holding a little child. Joe started and stepped back as he looked at it. "It is the baby in the watch," he said. "This must be where he lives, and that is his mother." Someone was coming. He was caught at last; he felt sure. He slid into a pew and crawled under the seat and kept very still--so still, in fact, that he fell asleep. When he awoke a light was burning in the church, and its rays fell across the picture of the mother and child in such a way that the eyes of the mother seemed to be looking straight at Joe under the seat.

For the first time in his life, he felt like crying. "I wish I had a mother," he thought, "and I should like to have her hold me in her arms just as that little boy's mother is holding him. I would tell her about this watch, and perhaps she would tell me how to get it back to the lady."

Joe crept from under the seat and stood up, and coming toward him down the aisle was a man. Joe thought he wore a queer-looking costume, and he dodged back of the seat; but the man had seen him, and there was no use in trying to run away; besides that, Joe was not at all sure that he wished to get away.

"Is this your house?" asked Joe when the man came up to him.

"No, my son," he replied; "this is the house of God."

Joe's heart leaped for joy; that was the name of the One the Salvation Army people told him about, who loved everybody and helped you.

"If you please," said Joe, "I should like to see Him."

The good man looked at Joe very earnestly, and then he said, "If you tell me what you wish to see Him about, I am sure I can help you."

Joe told him about the watch and that he felt sure the lady lived there, as the baby in the big picture was very much like the picture in the watch. "And if this is God's house," said Joe, "I thought He might be the father and forgive me. I am very sorry that I took it."

The good man took Joe by the hand. "Come with me," he said; "you are forgiven, I am sure."

Joe was given a good supper, and for the first time in his life, he slept in a real bed.

The next day the good man found the owner of the watch, and when she heard Joe's story, she forgave him.

Joe was placed in a school, where he learned to be a good boy, as well as to be studious, and he soon forgot the old life. He grew to be a man of whom any mother could have been proud. But the only mother Joe ever knew was the mother of the little boy in the picture, which he cherishes as a thing sacred in his life.

THE END

Section 6: SUSAN CAT AND THE WITCH

Once upon a time, there was a little girl named Betty. She was an orphan, and a bad landlord turned her out of her home. The only friend she had was a black cat named Susan. Betty was crying as she walked along the road, and Susan Cat ran beside her, rubbing against her feet. All at once, she ran in front of Betty and stood on her hind legs. "Do not cry, mistress," she said. "I'll take care of you."

Betty was so surprised to hear Susan Cat speak that she stopped crying at once. "You poor Susan Cat," she said, "what can you do? We must go to the city, and if I can find work we shall be able to live; if not, you must take care of yourself, for you can catch mice and keep from starving."

"You come with me, mistress," answered Susan Cat, "and you will not need to work, and you will not starve." And she put out her paw for Betty to take and walked alongside her. When they came to a path leading into the wood, Susan Cat led Betty along this path until they were in front of two very large trees which had grown together, but there was a big opening in the trunk. "We'll go in here," said Susan Cat, and as they stepped through, they were in a hall. She led Betty up the stairs to a room where there were a snowy-white bed and beautiful furnishings. "Dinner will be served as soon as you are dressed, mistress," said Susan Cat.

After she had gone, Betty looked around, and in the closets, she found pretty dresses which just fitted her. She put on one of them, and in a few minutes, she was ready for dinner. Just then she heard a soft, scratching noise at the door, and when she opened it, Susan Cat walked in.

"How do you like your new home, mistress?" she asked.

"Very much," Betty answered. "But we cannot live in such a nice house. We have no money, and, besides that, this house must belong to someone. And this dress I have on must belong to some little girl. I should not wear it."

"The dress did belong to a little girl," said Susan Cat, "but she cannot wear it now, and she wants you to have it.

And do not fret about the house. It belongs to me. I cannot tell you any more just now, but you need not worry anymore about anything, for you are to live here, if you wish, after you have dinner, for then you will meet a boy, and you may not like him."

Susan Cat led Betty into a room where the table was set for three persons, and when they were seated a boy about Betty's age came in and sat with them. He wore his hat, and a thick veil hung from it.

"I am sorry I cannot remove my hat," he said, in a lovely voice, "and I will go away if you'd rather I would."

"Oh no," said Betty, feeling very much like an intruder. "I am very grateful to you for letting me stay, and I will help to do the work."

"You do not need to work," said the boy. "If you will stay, we will be very glad."

Betty did not once get a glimpse of his face; he lifted the veil so carefully. And there sat Susan Cat, using her knife and fork like any lady. Betty smiled to herself when she thought of her eating from a saucer.

Suddenly Susan Cat slid out of her chair and crawled under it, and the little boy trembled so that his chair shook. Betty looked around to find the cause of their strange behavior and saw standing in the doorway an older woman with a staff in her hand. She hobbled over to where Susan Cat sat and raised the staff. Betty thought she was going to strike her.

"Don't you hurt Susan Cat!" she cried, running toward the old witch, who was so startled that she dropped the staff, and Betty picked it up.

"Don't let her have it again," said the boy; "that is the cause of all our trouble."

Betty threw the staff in a closet and locked the door. All this time, the witch was stepping backward toward the door by which she entered, and she grew smaller with each step. By the time she was out of the house, she had looked like a black speck, and a breeze blowing just then carried her out of sight. "But how shall we ever be ourselves again?" said the boy. "She has gone, and here we are, in this state."

"Perhaps the stick will do it," said Susan Cat.

Betty wondered what they meant, and the boy told her that Susan Cat was his sister before the witch changed her into a cat, and made his face so hideous that he had to wear a veil, and they had lived very happily together. "But one day the old witch came and wanted to live with us, and we let her for a while, but she was so cross and made us so unhappy we told her she must go away. Then she brought all this change upon us, and every once in a while, she returns and frightens us, for we do not know what she will change us into next."

"Let me get the stick," said Betty. "Perhaps we can change Susan Cat to your sister again."

Betty opened the door of the closet, and instead of the stick, there was a bright streak of light, and walking on it was a little Fairy who held a wand in her hand.

"You will soon be happy again," she told them. "I have destroyed the stick, and the old witch will never return."

Then she walked over to Susan Cat and touched her with her wand, and there stood a little girl about Betty's age in place of the black cat.

"Now close your eyes," said the Fairy, "for I want the boy to remove his veil, and his face is not pleasant to look upon."

Betty did as the Fairy told her, but I am sorry to tell you that she peeked a very little. Betty closed her eyes tight after the first glimpse and waited for the Fairy to say to her to open them again, and when she did, there stood the boy with a very smiling face.

His sister ran to him and put her arms around him. "Now we shall be happy," she said, "and Betty will live with us. How can we thank you?" she asked the Fairy.

"Oh, I shall be repaid by seeing you all happy," the Fairy replied. "And now I must go."

"Will we see you again?" asked Betty.

"No," answered the Fairy. "I only appear when people are in trouble, and you will never need me again."

THE END

CPSIA information can be obtained
at www.ICGtesting.com
Printed in the USA
BVHW041951230421
605736BV00015B/484

9 781801 836296